Dear Parent:
Your child's love of reading starts here!

Every child learns to read in a different way and at his or her own speed. Some go back and forth between reading levels and read favorite books again and again. Others read through each level in order. You can help your young reader improve and become more confident by encouraging his or her own interests and abilities. From books your child reads with you to the first books he or she reads alone, there are I Can Read Books for every stage of reading:

SHARED READING
Basic language, word repetition, and whimsical illustrations, ideal for sharing with your emergent reader

BEGINNING READING
Short sentences, familiar words, and simple concepts for children eager to read on their own

READING WITH HELP
Engaging stories, longer sentences, and language play for developing readers

READING ALONE
Complex plots, challenging vocabulary, and high-interest topics for the independent reader

ADVANCED READING
Short paragraphs, chapters, and exciting themes for the perfect bridge to chapter books

I Can Read Books have introduced children to the joy of reading since 1957. Featuring award-winning authors and illustrators and a fabulous cast of beloved characters, I Can Read Books set the standard for beginning readers.

A lifetime of discovery begins with the magical words "I Can Read!"

Visit www.icanread.com for information
on enriching your child's reading experience.

I Can Read Book® is a trademark of HarperCollins Publishers.

Pinkalicious Treasury

Pinkalicious: School Rules!
Pinkalicious: Pinkie Promise
Pinkalicious: The Princess of Pink Slumber Party
Pinkalicious: Fairy House
Pinkaliciousand the Cupcake Calamity
Pinkalicious: Tutu-rrific

Based on the HarperCollins book *Pinkalicious* written by Victoria Kann and Elizabeth Kann, illustrated by Victoria Kann
For information address HarperCollins Children's Books,
a division of HarperCollins Publishers,
195 Broadway, New York, NY 10007.
www.icanread.com

ISBN: 978-0-06-243636-8

October 2015

15 16 17 18 19 SCP 10 9 8 7 6 5 4 3 2 1

Pinkalicious®
Treasury

HARPER

An Imprint of HarperCollinsPublishers

Table of Contents

To Zelda, Grace, and David
—V.K.

The author gratefully acknowledges
the artistic and editorial contributions
of Daniel Griffo and Susan Hill.

Pinkalicious®

School Rules!

by Victoria Kann

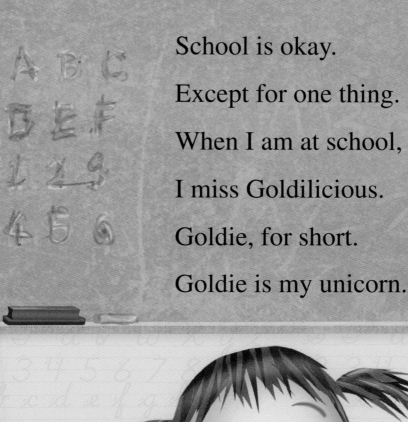

School is okay.

Except for one thing.

When I am at school,

I miss Goldilicious.

Goldie, for short.

Goldie is my unicorn.

I really like my teacher.

His name is Mr. Pushkin.

I have some friends in my class
and I made a new friend yesterday.
But I miss Goldie anyway.

This morning when I woke up

I had a very good idea.

I could bring Goldie to school with me!

School would be
perfectly pinkatastic
with Goldilicious
there, too.

There was a shiny red apple

on Mr. Pushkin's desk.

Goldie took the apple
and nibbled it gently.

Mr. Pushkin heard Goldie munching
and he thought it was me.
"Pinkalicious, there is no eating
until snack time," he said.
"It's the rule."

"It's not me," I said.

"It's Goldilicious, my unicorn!

She didn't eat much for breakfast,"

I added.

Mr. Pushkin smiled.

He took me aside

and he told me that unicorns

are not allowed in school.

"It's the rule," he said.

Rules are something

I do not love about school.

And I really do not love

the rule about no unicorns.

I began to cry a little.

I cried a little harder.

"Okay, Pinkalicious,"

said Mr. Pushkin.

"Your unicorn may stay,

just this once."

I stopped crying.

In fact, I clapped and twirled.

"But if your unicorn stays, you must teach her the rules," Mr. Pushkin said. "Do you think you can do that?"

"Yes!" I said.

"I know I can!"

At reading time,

Goldilicious was very quiet.

Goldilicious helped me with my math.

Unicorns are very good at counting.

When it was time for recess,

I showed Goldilicious

how to line up by the door.

Goldilicious did not push

or wiggle or cut the line at all.

Goldilicious played nicely

with the other kids.

Everyone had so much fun
with Goldie and me.

I didn't know I had

so many friends at school!

Soon it was time to go home.

Goldie got my backpack

off its hook.

"Tell me, Pinkalicious,"

said Mr. Pushkin.

"Did you and your unicorn

have a good day?"

"We sure did!" I said.

37

"School rules!"

Pinkalicious

Pinkie Promise

For Marjorie and Bob,
thank you for your support and guidance.
—V.K.

The author gratefully acknowledges
the artistic and editorial contributions
of Daniel Griffo and Susan Hill.

Pinkie Promise

by Victoria Kann

I was making a picture

for my teacher, Mr. Pushkin.

I ran out of my favorite color.

I asked my friend Alison

if I could borrow her paints.

"Just don't use up all the pink," she said.

"I won't," I said.

"I promise."

I worked very hard on the picture.

It looked good.

I gave the picture to Mr. Pushkin.

"What a terrific painting!" he said.

"It's so pink."

"You mean it's pinkerrific!" I said.

Alison was coming over
to get her paint set.

Some of the colors were empty.

Uh-oh.

What was I going to do?

"Um . . . I'm sorry, Alison," I said.

"By mistake I used up all the pink."

Alison frowned.

"You also used up all the red

and the white," she said.

"Well, red and white make pink,

so really it's all pink," I said.

Alison was angry.

"You said you wouldn't use up
all the pink paint!" said Alison.
"You promised."
"I'm really really sorry, Alison,"
I said again.
Alison took her paint set
and walked away.

Alison did not sit with me at lunch.

I sat alone.

I ate my jelly sandwich.

Jelly does not taste pink-a-yummy

if you are eating all by yourself.

Then I thought of something.

I went back to the classroom.

I made Alison a card to apologize.

"This card is very blue,"

I said to Alison.

"There were no other colors.

Almost everybody is out of pink."

"Thanks for the card," Alison said.

"It's not just beautiful, it's bluetiful."

"Alison," I asked,

"can we still be friends?"

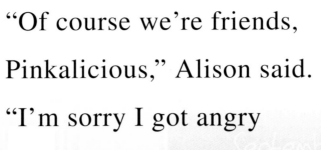

"Of course we're friends,
Pinkalicious," Alison said.
"I'm sorry I got angry
about the paint.
I won't get so mad next time."

I was so happy!

"Let's play this weekend!" I said.

When Alison came over to play,

I had a surprise for her.

I gave Alison a new tube of paint.

"It's not even my birthday!"

said Alison.

"And that's not all," I said.

"Guess what?"

We got ice cream!

We shared a pink peppermint ice cream sundae with raspberry swirl syrup.

The sundae had two cherries on top
so we could each have our own.
Some things are just too hard to share!

PLEASING POMEGRANATE PUNCH

MAGENTA MINT MANGO

PINK PEPPERMINT

PLUM PINK PERFECTION

"Let's always be friends,"
Alison said.

"Yes, that would be funtastic,"
I said.

"Let's make it a pinkie promise!"
we said at the same time.
"Pinkie promises last forever,"
I said happily.

Pinkalicious®

The Princess of Pink
Slumber Party

For Jennifer and Sydney
—V.K.

The author gratefully acknowledges
the artistic and editorial contributions
of Jared Osterhold and Natalie Engel.

The Princess of Pink
Slumber Party

by Victoria Kann

I was having a slumber party.

It was not any old slumber party.

It was a Princess of Pink party!

My whole family got ready.

Mommy and Daddy dressed up

like a queen and a king.

"I'm the royal prince," said Peter.

He grabbed a crown out of my hand.

"You're more like a royal joker,"
I told him.

DING DONG!

"The princesses are here!" I said.

I twirled my way to the door

and let my royal friends in.

"Welcome," I said with a curtsy.

"Enter the castle, fair maidens!"

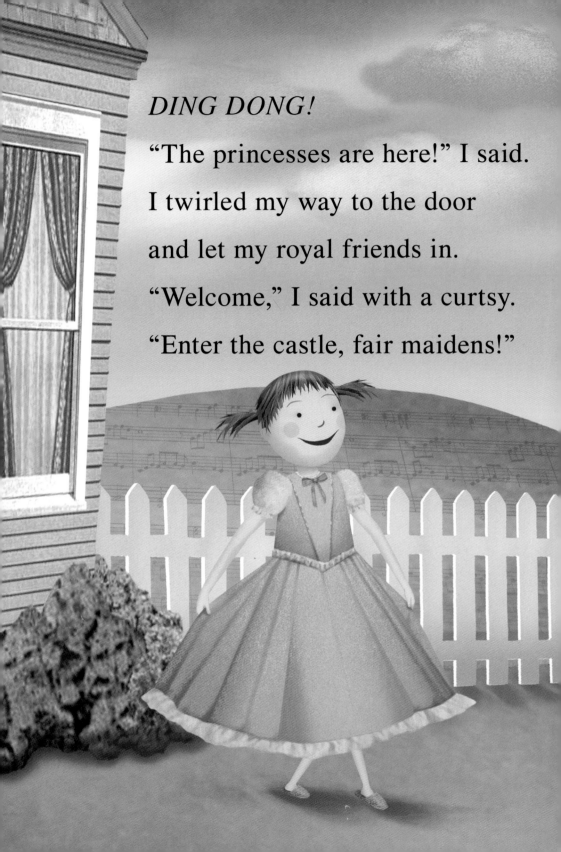

"How grand!" Molly said.

"I'm ready for the ball!" Rose said.

"Hello, Princess Alison," I said.

"Hi," Alison said quietly.

She held her bear tightly.

"Let's play musical thrones!"
I started the music
and we danced around the chairs.
I didn't even mind being
the last one left without a throne.

"Yay! I won!" said Molly.

"Your prize, Your Majesty," I said.

I handed Molly a pinkatastic wand.

"It's time to make tiaras!" I said.

"Ohhhh," Rose said.

"Look at the dazzling jewels!"

"My tiara is going to twinkle

like a star," said Molly.

"Look at me," I said.

I put my tiara proudly on my head.

"I have the sparkliest tiara
in all the land!"

"Dinner is served!" said Mommy.

"We made a royal feast," said Daddy.

"Princess-and-the-Split-Pea Soup,

Chicken Nuggets à la King,

and Castle Cupcakes for dessert!"

Peter said, "If I was ruler,

we'd always eat dessert first!"

"Yum," I said.

"That would be a very sweet kingdom!"

After dinner Peter climbed

to the top of a pile of pillows

and yelled, "I'm king of the castle!"

"It's princess of the castle
around here," I said.

"Princesses rule!" Molly said.

Suddenly I heard a sniffle.

It came from Alison.

"What's wrong?" I asked her.

"I'm scared to sleep over,"
she whispered in my ear.

I gave Alison a hug.

"Sleeping away from home
can be kind of scary," I said.

"What would a real princess do
to make Alison feel better?" I asked.
"Protect her from villains!" Rose said.
"A princess faces her perils
with strength," Molly said.
Alison still looked scared.

"I know!" I said.

"A real princess would have
a dragon to protect her!"

"Close your eyes," I said.

"Unlock the magic kingdom!

What do you see?"

"Nothing," said Alison.

90

"Listen!" I said.

"Do you hear the dragon
walking in the enchanted forest?"

"That's your dad walking down the hall,"
Rose said.

"Breathe!" I said.

"Do you smell the odor
of dragon breath in the air?"

"Oh, excuse me," Molly said.

"I just burped!"

"Wait!" I said.

"Don't you hear the loud beating
of the dragon's heart?"

"That is my heart," said Rose.

"I've never seen a dragon before!"

"Now open your eyes," I said.

"The dragon is here!

It is pink and it is breathing fire.

Look how spiky its tail is!"

"I see the dragon!" Alison said.

"It is sparkling in the moonlight."

The dragon smiled.

"She will protect us," I said.

"What do you think
the dragon's name is?" Rose asked.

Alison yawned.

"Can I tell you in the morning?
I'm so sleepy," Alison said.

"Goodnight, Princesses of Pink,"
I said.

"Goodnight, dragon," we all said.

Outside, the dragon winked.

Pinkalicious®

Fairy House

For Sydney!
xox,
Aunt Victoria

The author gratefully acknowledges
the artistic and editorial contributions
of Daniel Griffo and Natalie Engel.

Fairy House

by Victoria Kann

It was spring,

my favorite season.

I love how the sky looks like

cotton candy at sunset.

Every spring, our garden comes alive
with blossoms of every color.
I know why our garden
is so beautiful.
It's because of the fairies!

Fairies come to our yard

and sprinkle fairy dust

to make the plants grow.

I have never seen them,

but I know that they are real.

I can see sparkles outside my window.

This spring, I had a plan.

I would see the fairies!

"Pinkalicious, what are you doing?"

asked Peter as I collected

twigs and leaves.

"I'm making a house

for the fairies to live in.

Then they can live in our garden

and we will be able to see them,"

I said.

"I want to see them, too!

Let me help," said Peter.

He brought out his shell collection.

"Let's build the house here

in the garden," I said.

"Fairies are sure to come this way."

Piece by piece,
we built a little house.
I wove buttercups
around the door.
Peter made a pathway
with his shells.

Soon we had a cozy home
for the fairies.

I couldn't wait for them to come.

Every day I watched the house

from my swing.

I made a pond, a boat,

and even a slide

for the fairies to find.

But the fairies did not come.

When Peter saw how sad I looked
he said, "Cheer up—the pink flower buds
are blooming!"
But I wanted to see the fairies!

Suddenly, I had an idea.

"Maybe the fairies only come out
at night," I said.

"Maybe they only sprinkle fairy dust
by moonlight!"

I told Mommy and Daddy

what I wanted to do.

They let Peter and me camp out

and keep watch for the fairies.

That evening, Peter and I
spread out our sleeping bags.
I left the fairies a sweet snack
of honeysuckle and berries.

"Do you think they will come?"
asked Peter.

"Yes," I said,

and added in a whisper,

"I really, really hope so."

We told each other stories
until Peter fell asleep.
As the night got darker
I heard crickets and owls,
but not a single fairy.

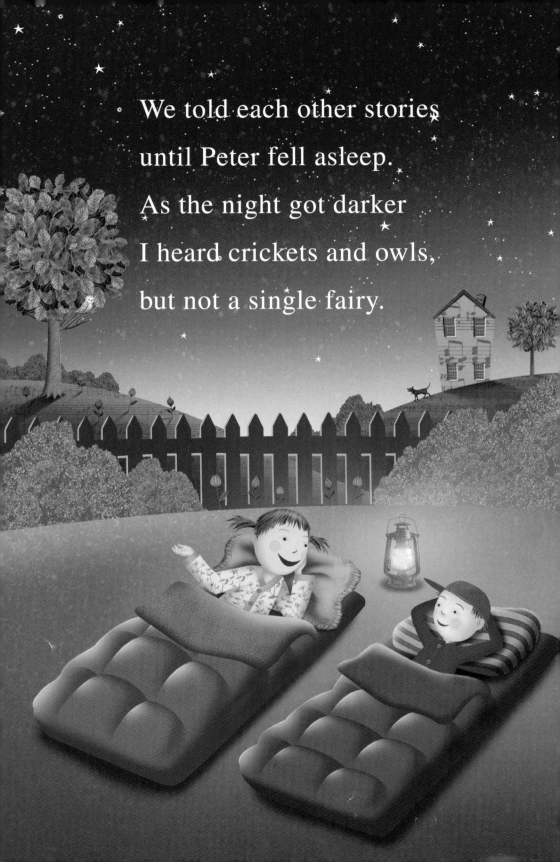

Once I thought I heard

some soft, gentle humming.

It was just Peter.

He was snoring.

I did everything I could
to stay awake.
I looked up at the moon.
I counted the stars.
I didn't want to miss the fairies.

120

But as I counted the stars,
my eyelids got heavy.
I couldn't help it.
I drifted off to sleep.

The next thing I knew,

I heard a bird singing.

I opened my eyes.

It was dawn.

I heard hushed voices in the garden.

Mommy and Daddy

were looking at something together.

"How beautiful!" they said.

As I stretched,

a sweet smell filled the air.

All around me,

colorful flowers were in full bloom.

I looked at the fairy house.

The honeysuckle and berries

were gone.

"The fairies came!" I cried.

"They came,

but I missed the whole thing."

Peter started to sniffle.

"Don't cry. Look!" I said.

Up in the air

I could see glimmers of light

shooting across

the early-morning sky.

"Fairies." I gasped.

The light shimmered

brighter and brighter

until it sparkled into sunshine.

"I knew you were real," I said.

127

My family and I

watched the sun come up.

"Thank you, fairies," I whispered.

Wherever they were,

I knew they could hear me.

Pinkalicious®

and the Cupcake Calamity

For Sophia

—V.K.

The author gratefully acknowledges
the artistic and editorial contributions
of Robert Masheris and Natalie Engel.

and the Cupcake Calamity

by Victoria Kann

One Sunday morning,

we saw a huge crowd outside

Mr. Swizzle's ice cream shop.

I stopped to see what was happening.

"Step right up, folks,"
Mr. Swizzle called.
Behind him was a pink curtain.

"Prepare your taste buds,"
said Mr. Swizzle.
"Dessert is about to be served!"
He lifted the curtain.
The crowd gasped.

Right in front of me was the biggest,
fanciest machine in the world!
Lights were flashing.
Gears were turning.
It hummed, buzzed, and beeped.

"Behold," said Mr. Swizzle,
"my Cupcake-Create-O-Matic!
Just add a dollar and your cupcake
will bake right on the spot!"
I couldn't wait to try it.

BUZZ

HUMM HUMM

BEEP BEEP

Ice Cream

"Me first!" I said.

I ran to the machine

and put in my dollar.

I chose a strawberry cupcake

with pink frosting and pink sprinkles.

I pressed the green button.

Nothing happened.

"Bake!" I said, pressing again.

But no cupcake came out.

"Let me try," said Alison.
One after the other,
people put their money in.
But nothing came out.

"What's going on here?"

The crowd started to grumble.

People were getting upset.

So was I.

I wanted my cupcake!

"I'm so sorry," said Mr. Swizzle.

"Let me get the owner's guide.

I'll have this fixed in a jiffy."

I couldn't wait that long.

I wanted a pink cupcake!

Hmmm . . . I thought.

I looked hard at the machine.

I walked around to the back.

There was a little door

big enough to squeeze through.

So I did!

The Cupcake-Create-O-Matic
was amazing inside!
Mixing bowls whirred
as batter stirred.
Sprinkles and frosting
drizzled everywhere.

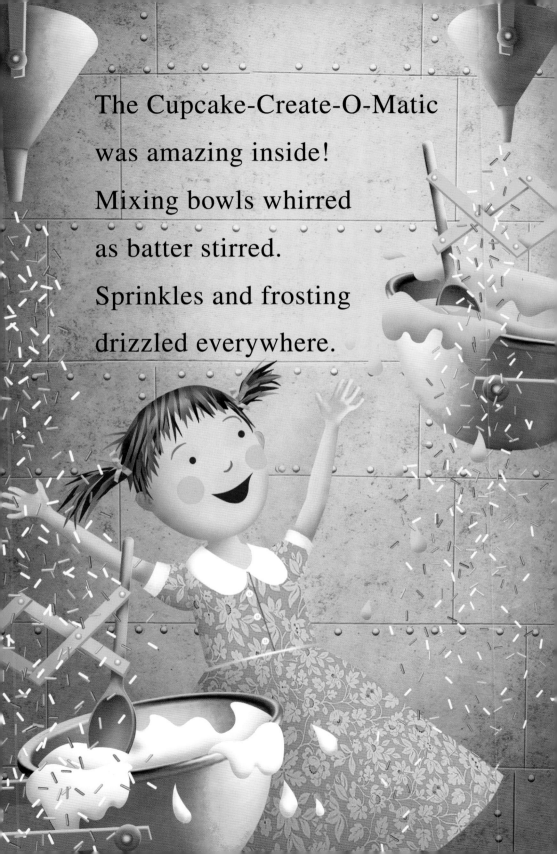

I started poking around.

The batter was blending nicely.

It tasted good, too.

There were belts full of
cupcake wrappers,
all ready to be filled.
I swapped out the plain ones
for ones with polka dots.

Then I saw that
only half of the machine
was working.
The mixers weren't pouring batter
into the wrappers.

"There must be a power switch
in here somewhere,"
I said to myself.
I looked up and there it was!

The switch was way up

at the top of the machine.

I climbed all the way there.

"It's cupcake time!" I said

as I flipped it on.

The Cupcake-Create-O-Matic
started rumbling right away.
In fact, it started rattling.
Then, it started shaking.
"Uh-oh," I said.

The machine started filling up
with batter!
"I want to eat a cupcake," I said,
"not BE a cupcake!"

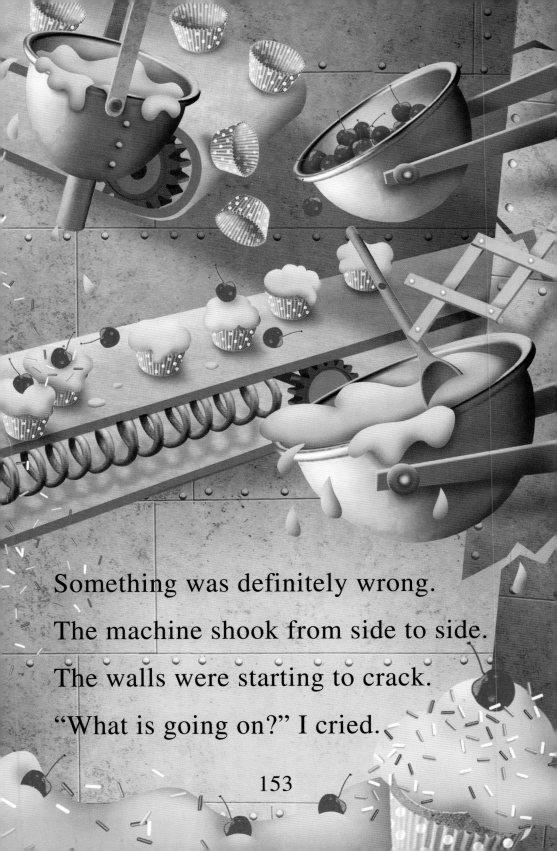

Something was definitely wrong.

The machine shook from side to side.

The walls were starting to crack.

"What is going on?" I cried.

BOOM!

The next thing I knew,

I was outside again.

The walls of the machine

had fallen down around me.

I was sitting on top
of the world's biggest cupcake.

"Pinkalicious!" cried Mr. Swizzle.

"What are you doing up there?

Are you okay?"

I blinked. I smiled.

"Yes. I am perfect!

In fact, I couldn't be better,"

I said.

The crowd roared with laughter.

Mr. Swizzle looked relieved.

"Dig in, everyone!" he said.

Everyone loved the giant treat.

"Sorry about your machine,"
I told Mr. Swizzle.
"That's okay, Pinkalicious," he said.
"From now on, I'll stick to ice cream
and leave the cupcakes to you!"

Pinkalicious®

Tutu-rrific

For Lilly
—V.K.

The author gratefully acknowledges the artistic and
editorial contributions of Daniel Griffo and Natalie Engel.

Tutu-rrific

by Victoria Kann

Alison and I giggled as we tried
to balance on our toes.
Tomorrow we were going
to ballet class together!
I was pink with glee.

I had never taken
a ballet class before,
but Alison had.
"You'll love it," she said.
"We twirl and jump through the air
and spin on our tippy-toes."
"What fun!" I said.

"What's your outfit like?" I asked.

"It's a purple tutu,"

said Alison.

"What does yours look like?"

I laughed and said, "Guess!"

The next day, I got ready:

I wore my pink tutu,

pink slippers,

and pink bows in my hair.

Mommy took me to class.

When we got there, I thought I saw

a purple tutu.

"There's Alison!" I said.

I ran inside to catch Alison.

There were people all over!

I thought I saw a flash of purple

run into a room.

"Alison, wait!" I called.

But Alison didn't hear me.

I followed her into the class.

I couldn't spot her

with all the dancers.

Just then, the teacher walked in.

"Okay, everyone!" she said.

"Take your place at the barre."

I'd have to find Alison later.

"Time to warm up," said the teacher.

"First position," she called.

I looked around the room.

Everyone was moving their feet.

Heels together, toes apart.

This was easy!

"Plié," the teacher sang.

The ballerinas bent their knees,

so I did, too.

Piece of cake!

"Very good," said the teacher.

"Now, let's go over

the dance we learned last week."

I didn't know the moves,

but I wasn't worried.

Ballet seemed really, really simple.

The teacher put on some music.

The dancers moved their arms,

first up, then down.

Then they kicked their legs

up and down.

I followed along just fine.

Suddenly, the music got faster.

The girls skipped in a circle

and jumped in the air.

I was stuck in the middle,

not sure what to do.

Everyone moved so quickly.

I couldn't keep up!

When I hopped, they kicked.

When I kicked, they swayed.

"Hold on!" I cried.

But no one could hear me!

I looked around for Alison,

but she wasn't there.

It was a girl who looked like Alison.

I had made a mistake.

I knew I had to say something.

I stopped dancing and raised my hand.

"Excuse me," I said.

"I think I'm in the wrong class!"

Just as I put my hand up,

the dancers jumped up high.

"Beautiful!" said the teacher.

She didn't see me!

I tried to get out of the circle,

but the dancers linked arms.

I tried crawling through their legs,

but the dancers hopped up and down.

"Wait!" I shouted,
but nothing helped.
I was trapped between tutus
with no way out.

"Get ready for the grand finale!"
the teacher called out.

I gulped.

The girls spread out their arms
and started twirling.

"Oh!" I said, happily surprised.

They were spinning!

I could do this!

I took a deep breath

and twirled and whirled

and spun around.

I was spinning so freely,
I didn't notice that everyone
had stopped.

The teacher looked at me, confused.

"You!" she said.

"You're not in this class!"

"Uh-oh," I whispered.

I was sure I was in trouble.

Instead, the teacher just smiled.

"You must be in the wrong room,"
she said.

"I'll have someone walk you to
the beginner class.

But first, could you spin again?"

I twirled around once more.

"You're so graceful!" said the teacher.

"Keep practicing and soon

you will be in my advanced class."

In the beginner class,

I told Alison what happened.

"What was it like?" she asked.

"It was tutu-rrific!" I said,

and did a pirouette.